MOIN
THE MONSTER
SONGSTER

Read more by Anushka Ravishankar from Duckbill
Moin and the Monster

Other books by Anushka Ravishankar
Tiger on a Tree
Catch That Crocodile
Elephants Never Forget
One Two Tree!
Today Is My Day
Excuse Me, Is This India?
Wish You Were Here
To Market! To Market!
The Fivetongued Firefanged Folkadotted Dragon Snake
Alphabets Are Amazing Animals
Anything but a Grabooberry
I Like Cats
Excuses! Excuses!
Song of the Bookworm
Where's the Baby Gone?
The Rumour
The Boy Who Drew Cats
The Monkeys and the Capseller
The Shepherd Boy
The Goose That Laid Golden Eggs
The Fox and the Crow
The Hare and the Tortoise
The Storyteller: Tales from the Arabian Nights
Zain and Ana: At Least a Fish
Zain and Ana: Ghosts Don't Eat
Zain and Ana: Just Like a Bug
Puppets Unlimited with Everyday Materials
Toys and Tales with Everyday Materials
Masks and Performance with Everyday Materials
Trash! On Ragpicker Children and Recycling

MOIN THE MONSTER SONGSTER

Anushka Ravishankar

Illustrations by
Anitha Balachandran

duckbill

Duckbill Books

Venkat Towers, 165, P.H. Road, Maduravoyal
Chennai 600 095
www.duckbill.in
platypus@duckbill.in

First published by Duckbill Books 2012

10 9 8 7 6 5 4 3 2 1

ISBN: 978-93-81626-91-7

Typeset by Ram Das Lal
Lettering for *The Monster Rule Book*
by Vani Malhotra

Printed at Thomson Press (India) Ltd.

Also available as an ebook

Children's reading levels vary widely. The general reading
levels are indicated by colour on the back cover. There are
three levels: younger readers, middle readers and young
adult readers. Within each level, the position of the dot
indicates the reading complexity. Books for young
adults may contain some slightly mature material.

HOW MOIN GOT A MONSTER

One night, in the dim darkness of his room, Moin heard something shuffling and sniffling under his bed.

It was a monster, but Moin could not see it until he drew it. So the monster described itself, and Moin drew it.

The monster was most displeased. 'I'm supposed to be fearsome!' it complained. 'You've made me look funny!'

Moin was very annoyed at having his drawing criticised. 'I didn't ask you to hide under my bed and wake me up in the middle of the night,' he sulked.

But Moin and the monster were stuck together, because of the monster rules.

And it looked like they would have to stay together forever.

Eyes like flames
And nose like pails
Ears like horns
And teeth like nails
A scary, fearsome sight to see
Monster, monster, monster me!

Skull-shaped mole
On rock-like chin
Long green hair
And purple skin
In the dark you'll scream to see
Monster, monster, monster ME!

Drum-shaped chest
And arms like trees
Bamboo legs on
Feet like skis
Terrifying as can be
Monster, monster, monster
MEEEEEEEEEEE!

THE COLOUR PURPLE

'You haven't told me any new rules in a long time,' Tony complained to the monster.

Tony was trying to write two books at the same time. He had started off with *The Monster Rule Book*. But he was also writing *The Strange Behaviour of Monsters*. Since the monster always behaved strangely, this book was much thicker than the *Rule Book*.

The monster couldn't remember all the rules. Whenever it remembered one suddenly, Tony wrote it down. The monster also remembered them in random order, so Tony had more gaps than rules.

'Ha. Rules, my left toe,' Moin muttered. He was convinced the monster was making up the rules.

'I told you there's a rule about making rules,' the monster said.

'It's true,' said Tony. 'See rule number 18.'

'Ha. Number 18 my purple toenail,' muttered Moin.

'Hey! I want to paint my toenails purple!'

'You don't have toenails,' Moin pointed out.

'And whose fault is that?' asked the monster. 'Did I ask you to make my feet look like brooms? Now the least you can do is help these ugly broom-feet look pretty. I can paint the edges purple.'

'Purple! Such an ugly colour!' said Moin.

The monster stood on top of Moin's bed and scowled. 'Purple is the best colour in the world! I was supposed to be purple, and you made me pink. Just because you didn't have a purple crayon,' it added bitterly. 'I would have looked magnificent in purple. Now I look like a … like a … baby's bottom!'

'My baby cousin's bottom is not pink, it's brown,' said Moin.

The monster sighed. 'You're missing the point. As usual.' He turned to Tony. 'You tell me. Wouldn't I have totally rocked in deep purple?'

'You look very nice in pink,' said Tony, who thought the monster was the best thing that had ever happened. He was glad it had chosen

MONSTER

BY TONY SINGH

RULE BOOK

Monster rule 1

Every monster has to obey the monster rules Without

asking any awkward Questions.

Monster rule 7

A monster can eat anything it wants.

Monster rule 4

A monster is neither masculine nor feminine.

Monster rule 17

A monster can be sent to human world.

Monster rule 18

A monster cannot make up rules.

~~Monster rule 12~~

Monster rule 42

When a monster is sent to human world, It has t
hide under the bed. If there is no bed, It can hid
under a cupoard or any other suitable peice of furni
If there is no peice of suitable furniture, It should l
for a dark corner.

Monster rule 54

A monster has to stay ~~for~~ forever with the
human who has given it a body. (Also see rules
numbers 71, 228 and 364).

Monster Rule 47

A monster can alter it's ~~appearance~~ appearance
with in reasonable limits.

Monster rule 64

While travelling in the human world, a monste
can flatten and fold itself to fit into a small
space

Monster rule 93

A monster cannot get rid of any bodily part:
it ~~aqu~~ acquires in the human world.

Monster rule 112

Food fit for humans is not always fit for
monsters

Monster rule 114

A monster cannot be gifted away

Monster Rule 321

Human products can have unpredictable side effect
on monsters.

Moin's bed to hide under, though. Tony didn't think he could have dealt with its singing and its appetite for bananas.

But the monster was looking really sad about being pink.

'Maybe we can change your colour,' said Tony, feeling sorry for it. 'Is there a monster rule that says you can't? If you could grow your hair, you could change your colour, surely. They're both enhancements.'

The monster yawned.

'Big word,' it said.

'Oh,' said Tony. He had forgotten that big words made the monster sleepy. 'What I mean,' he explained, 'is that Monster Rule 47 says that "a monster can alter its appearance within reasonable limits." That means you can change how you look up to a point. So maybe you can change your colour to purple.'

Moin looked up in alarm from the car he was making with matchboxes and the wheels he got from a packet of chips.

'Change its colour?' he cried. 'Oh no!'

'Change my colour!' cried the monster. 'Oh yes!'

'You know what happens when we try to do anything like that. You'll grow huge or become tiny or something!' said Moin. 'You don't even

remember the rules properly, so you never
know what can happen. Forget it!'

But the monster was already dancing
around in excitement and doing somersaults
on the table and singing in its shrieky voice:

I'll be purple, purple, purple plue
Not pink or green or ghastly blue
Not red or white or pale yellue
But purple, purple, purple plue!

Moin grabbed the monster, stuffed it in the
cupboard and shut the door.

Tony looked at him in alarm.

'I'm not allowed to sing!' Moin said, red and
panting with the exertion of dealing with a
wriggling, singing monster.

'Oh right!' said Tony.

He had forgotten about the disastrous
concert.

Escape Artist

Moin was in disgrace and had been banned from singing for a month. It was no great hardship for Moin to stop singing, but stopping the monster was proving to be an impossible task.

The trouble was that when the monster sang, Moin's parents thought it was Moin.

It had taken great courage for Moin's parents to send out invitations to family and friends to come to Moin's concert. Moin's teacher, Tothogotho Chowdhury had told them that Moin was his star student and would begin and end the concert, even though he was the youngest of his students.

Moin's father was so surprised, he gurgled in reply.

Moin's mother, who had also been

speechless for a moment, recovered quickly. 'That is wonderful, Chowdhuryji,' she said, though the words stuck in her throat and came out sounding strangled.

Tothogotho Chowdhury smiled benignly. He was used to parents getting emotional about their child's talent.

But Mr and Mrs Kaif's emotion was not what Tothogotho thought it was. For the past few months they had been alarmed by the strange noises that came from Moin's room. It pained them to hear their son sing such terrible songs in such a shrieky voice, but they endured it, because they were good, supportive parents. They even praised Moin for practising so much, because there was nothing else they could praise him for. Their stock of cotton wool was getting over rather rapidly, but apart from that they showed no outward signs of their misery.

So when they heard that Moin was going to be the star of the singing class concert, the emotion they felt was mainly amazed horror.

'G … g … g …' said Moin's father.

'He means, good for Moin,' said Mrs Kaif, sticking a sharp elbow into Mr Kaif's ribs.

'Ow!' yelled Mr Kaif, suddenly finding his voice.

'Please call all your friends and your family.

You will be so proud to hear Moin. I have not heard any child with such a pure, sweet voice in a long time.'

'Pure?' whispered Mrs Kaif hoarsely.

'Sweet?' Mr Kaif asked Mrs Kaif on the way home. 'I mean, I know he's our son and we should encourage him and all that, but … sweet?'

'Do you think we should get our ears examined?' asked Mrs Kaif. 'Maybe we're missing something.'

'I think it's that Chowdhury who's missing something,' muttered Mr Kaif. 'A screw, probably.'

Mrs Kaif had to agree he had a point. By no stretch of imagination could the voice that they heard from Moin's room be called sweet. Or pure, for that matter. But Chowdhury was known to be one of the best gurus in Hindustani classical music—surely he ought to know what he was talking about.

So, feeling puzzled, worried and rather miserable, they wrote out invitations to their friends and family. Moin's teachers and principal K.K. Kuttykrishnan (known to students as Kooki) were invited, and so were all his classmates and their parents.

'Luckily, there's a cricket match on that day,' said Mrs Kaif, as she wrote the last invitation.

'Why's it lucky?' asked Moin, who was on his way to the kitchen to get the monster some guava juice, which it had suddenly taken a liking to.

Mrs Kaif gulped. 'Lucky? Did I say luckily?' she said quickly. 'No, I meant unluckily, of course. Many people will stay home to watch cricket, and won't come to the concert. That's *un*lucky. Not lucky, not at all!' She felt so guilty that she swore that she would not pretend to have a headache and miss the concert, a thought that had crossed her mind once or twice.

On the day of the concert, Mr and Mrs Kaif went to the green room behind the stage to wish Moin luck.

'Why're you wearing a hat?' Moin asked his father.

'Er … um … I wanted to look smart for your concert, heh heh,' said Mr Kaif, pushing his dark glasses deep into his pocket so Moin wouldn't notice them. With a hat and dark glasses on, he was pretty sure he wouldn't be recognised.

'You look weird,' said Moin and went off to get ready.

There was plenty of time before the concert was to begin. Mr and Mrs Kaif saw Chowdhuryji at the door and were about to slink away, but he saw them.

'Come, come!' he cried. 'Welcome our guests with me.'

Mr Kaif was about to put on his glasses, but decided it might look very odd to welcome people looking like a spy. So he reluctantly put them in his pocket, and took off his hat. A piece of paper flew out of it.

'Where did that come from?' asked Mrs Kaif, watching the paper flutter away and fall between people's feet. 'You should pick it up.'

But when Mr Kaif trotted off to look for it, the paper was nowhere to be seen.

'Very strange,' muttered Mr Kaif, wandering back to join his wife. He brightened on seeing Kartar Singh, Tony's father. Tony had come too, and rushed away to meet Moin before he went on stage.

Parvati was already there.

'I'm telling you, I saw it!' she was telling Moin.

MONSTER RULE 64

While travelling in the human world, a monster can flatten and fold itself to fit into a small space.

'But I locked it up in my room,' said Moin. 'What happened?' asked Tony.

Parvati told him that she had seen the monster darting towards the dressing room.

'What if someone saw it and captured it?' asked Tony, alarmed.

'I wish,' said Moin. 'But it's impossible. How could it have got out of my room?'

'You must have forgotten to lock it,' said Parvati. 'You're such a sieve-brain.'

'Oh,' said Tony, 'Your mother told me to give you this.' He gave Moin his water bottle.

'Oh no!' groaned Moin. 'My water bottle

was in my room, which means my mother opened the door, which means the monster must have—'

'Escaped!' said the monster, striking a striking pose. It was wearing a flowing, bright green scarf and had stuck a string of flowers behind its ear.

From the other room, they could hear a girl's voice wailing, 'Who took my flowers?' and another one yelling, 'Hey! Someone stole my scarf!'

'I'm like Mussolini,' the monster smirked.

'Huh?' asked Moin.

'That chap who could escape from anywhere,' the monster explained. 'You don't know anything.'

'Oh! He means Houdini,' said Tony, who always knew everything. 'He was a magician.'

'Just like me,' said the monster. 'Though of course, he couldn't sing like me. How do I look? I want to make sure I make a good impression.'

'What impression? On whom? You go sit

with Tony in the audience, and stay quiet,' said Moin. He knew the monster found it difficult to control itself when it heard singing, which is why he had left it behind in spite of its loud protests.

'It's a good thing I'm such a good magician. No one saw me jump into the hat. By the way, your father needs to use a better shampoo. All that sweat. Blechh!' The monster shook itself like a dog after a bath.

There was a sudden commotion in the main green room. Tothogotho Chowdhury had arrived backstage, and the singers were all being given last-minute instructions and an encouraging talk.

'I have to go!' said Moin. 'Tony, Parvati, take it with you and make sure it behaves, okay?'

'Okay!' said Tony, happily.

'Don't worry, Moin. I'll take care of it,' said Parvati firmly.

She turned to grab the monster, but it was gone. A string of flowers and a scarf lay in a pile where it had been standing.

'Just like Houdini!' said Tony, in admiration.

KOOKI SEES THINGS

Principal K.K. Kuttykrishnan (known to his students as Kooki) was not sure he wanted to do this. He liked music; and he even sang sometimes, when he had had a good meal and was feeling pleased with life.

But to have to sit and listen for an hour while a bunch of children sang classical music was not something he looked forward to on a Sunday evening. Unfortunately, Tothogotho Chowdhury was his wife's best friend's classmate's brother. So his wife had insisted that they go.

'Tothogothoji told Indira that there's a boy in his class who is going to be a brilliant singer one day. And he's in your school, Sir. We have to go. The boy should get encouragement from you.'

Kooki's wife always called him 'Sir'. This was because before they were married, they had taught together for many years in a school, where all the teachers called each other 'Teacher' and 'Sir'. So although they had been married for more than twenty years, Kooki still called his wife 'Teacher' and she still called him 'Sir'.

'It's Sunday evening, Teacher. I'll miss my movie,' sulked Kooki. But he knew that once his wife had made up her mind there was nothing he could do.

The first person he saw when he got there was his psychiatrist, Dr Reddy. Kooki ducked behind his wife. He had missed his last appointment with the doctor. He had only gone to him once, when he had seen a strange pink creature in his room. Dr Reddy had asked him to come again. But since the vision had not reappeared, Kooki had decided that he would not go back.

He wondered what the psychiatrist was doing at the concert. He didn't seem to be the type who enjoyed music. In fact, the last time he met him, Kooki had sung the school anthem to him. Dr Reddy had shown no appreciation at all. He had looked somewhat stunned, but he had not said a single complimentary word. Clearly a philistine, who didn't understand music. Kooki scowled and ducked even lower, because Dr Reddy seemed to be looking his way.

'Stop pulling my pallu, Sir,' said Kooki's wife, fondly. She turned around. 'Why are you facing that side? We have to go this side.'

Kooki had never told his wife about the pink creature or the session with the psychiatrist, because he knew that if he did, she would send him off for a round of ayurvedic massages. It was her answer to everything and he detested those oily massages. So now he couldn't tell her why he was hiding.

'Unh, I … I'm going backstage. I thought we should go and wish the boy best of luck, no?'

Kooki's wife beamed. 'That is a very good thought, Sir!' she said. So they went towards the green rooms.

It was when they were about to enter that Kooki saw it again. A pink creature was trotting out of one of the green rooms.

'Aiyee!' he shouted, stopping mid-stride. Taken by surprise, Mrs Kooki walked into him.

'Uff!' she shouted, her face buried somewhere near Kooki's armpit. As a result, she didn't see the pink creature running

between Kooki's legs. It ducked under her sari.

Kooki was still gulping and swallowing when Parvati came dashing out, followed by Tony and Moin.

When they saw their principal, they stopped, dumbfounded.

Parvati was the only one who recovered her voice. 'G … good evening sir,' she said.

'Glug,' said Moin.

Tony was staring, for some reason, at Mrs Kooki's feet, and didn't say anything.

'You! Boeing! And Parvati! What are you doing here?'

'Moin is going to sing, sir!' said Parvati. She had noticed from the corner of her eye that Tony was pointing at Mrs Kooki's feet. She glanced quickly and saw what the boys were staring at. There was a strand of green hair trailing out from under Mrs Kooki's yellow sari. As usual, she would have to keep the adults distracted. She took a deep breath to launch into a long story, but she need not have bothered.

'Moin!' exclaimed Mrs Kooki. 'That's the boy Tothogothoji told Indira about! Which of you is Moin?'

'Eh?' said Moin absently. He had vaguely heard his name, but his attention was riveted on the pink near Mrs Kooki's feet.

Kooki pulled at Mrs Kooki pallu. 'Shh, Teacher. This is the boy I told you about. The one with the name like an aeroplane. He's ...' and Kooki rolled his eyes and shook his head from side to side vigorously.

Unfortunately for Kooki, that was the moment Dr Reddy came around the corner.

He saw Kooki making strange faces and shouted, 'Everyone, stand back! This man is my patient!'

Before anyone could react, he had jumped on Kooki, dropped him to the ground, and pinned his arms behind him, in one smooth movement.

Kooki was too winded to do anything, but Mrs Kooki was not going to stand around and watch her husband being treated in this way. She hit Dr Reddy on the head with her handbag. Since her handbag contained a bottle of water and a hardbound pocket edition of the *Oxford English Dictionary*, it was quite a lethal weapon.

'Owowowow!' yelled Dr Reddy.

Kooki, now released from the doctor's stranglehold, rolled over, and sat up just in time to see a pink creature scuttle out from under his wife's sari.

'Pink thing!' he shouted, pointing with a trembling finger. 'Did you see that, Teacher? Did you see that, doctor? Wasn't it a pink alien-monster-demon-like thing? Hunh? Hunh?'

Dr Reddy's head was still spinning from the hard knock, but he was not one of India's top psychiatrists for nothing. Ignoring the little birds going tweet in his ears and the stars bursting before his eyes, he sat up and asked Kooki in his gentlest voice, 'Why don't *you* tell me?'

OFF STAGE

'Where's Moin?' asked Tothogotho Chowdhury.

He looked around. There were three minutes before the curtain was to go up and Moin was nowhere to be seen.

'He was here right now,' said the girl who had lost her scarf. Her name was Mina.

'I saw him running out with his friends,' said another girl, who had a long name that no one could pronounce. It was something that sounded like Bhagyavaidyashala. No one quite believed that that could be a real name so they called her Colander instead, because someone had heard her mother call her that.

'Running out?' asked Tothogotho, frowning. 'Running out, when it's time to go on stage? That is very bad.'

'Maybe he went to the toilet, Masterji,' suggested a boy who was sometimes called Tamarind. His name was actually Imtiaz, but he forgot to cross the t once, so he went from Imtiaz to Imli, in a day. He was now known as Imli to some and Tamarind to others.

A long 'aaah' went round the room when Imli said this. A sudden urge to go to the toilet just before curtains up was completely understandable.

'But, but,' said a small boy called Bipin, and stopped. He wanted to say that the toilet was right next to the room in which they were, but he didn't want to get people worried. He decided to go to the toilet himself instead. He was a little worried about his performance and wanted to practise one note of his song all alone.

As he entered the loo, he heard a strange scuttling near the window. He looked up and saw a piece of paper slip through the window slats and fall to the floor. He picked it up. It was some kind of drawing.

He wondered who could have put it in. Why would anyone slip a drawing of a strange, pink, weird-looking creature into the loo?

He decided to investigate. He climbed up on to the toilet seat and peered out of the window. Three children were standing there,

looking up at the window. One of them was Moin.

'Bipin!' he yelled when he saw him. 'Did a pink thing come in there?'

'A pink piece of paper just fell into the bathroom,' said Bipin, waving the paper to show Moin. 'But Moin, come soon! Everyone is searching for you.'

'I'm coming,' said Moin. 'But hold on to that paper, okay? Hold it tight. Don't let it go, okay, Bipin? I'm coming!'

'Okay,' said Bipin. He got off the toilet seat, still holding on to the paper. The picture was really interesting. He smiled at the funny looking thing. It smiled back.

'Aaaah!' yelled Bipin. He seemed to be imagining things! How could a paper face smile back at him?

Someone knocked at the door. 'Come on, Bipin! We're going on stage now.'

Bipin realised he hadn't practised his difficult note. 'Coming!' he shouted back. Then he cleared his throat and sang the note that he felt he needed to get right.

Kaaga re kaaga re …

Suddenly the paper in his hand quivered,

and sang (if that sort of thing can be called singing):

Caw caw caw caw caw caw
That's the way the crows sing
Caw caw caw caw caw caw
They caw caw caw at everything.

Bipin screamed, dropped the paper and ran out of the toilet, to find that all the children were trooping out. At the same moment, Moin, Parvati and Tony came galloping up.

'Where's the mon … er … paper?' asked Moin, panting.

But Bipin was in a state of terror and could say nothing except 'Gah!'

The monster had scooted out with the other children, heading for the stage.

'Oh no!' Moin shouted and dashed off. The monster was weaving its way through the line of children. They were all so nervous and focused on the performance that they didn't notice a pink thing streaking past their feet.

Just as the monster was about to reach the stage, Moin dived to the ground and caught hold of it. He held it tight, and lay there winded. When he looked up he saw

Tothogotho Chowdhury looking down at him. Moin had landed near his feet.

Tothogotho was moved to tears. He held Moin by the shoulders and stood him up.

'No need to touch my feet, my boy, my blessings are always with you. You gave me a few minutes of anxiety, but I should have trusted you. May success always be yours. Come, we shall begin the programme.'

As he turned towards the stage, Moin turned around to look for Parvati and Tony, so he could hand over the struggling monster to them. But they hadn't been allowed past the stage door. He stood there for a moment wondering what to do.

'Stop squeezing me,' said the monster. 'What do you think I am? Orange squash?'

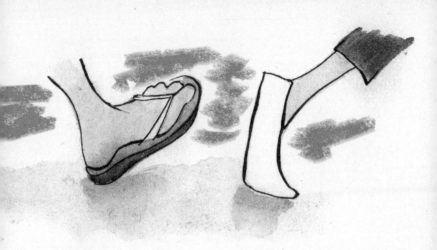

'Orange squash is not …' Moin began. 'Uff! Why am I trying to explain things to you? Look what a mess you've got me in. What am I to do with you?'

'Why should you do anything with me? I may have to stay with you but I don't belong to you. There's a monster rule about that.'

'How come all the monster rules are rules that suit you? Why isn't there a single rule that helps me? I wish there was a rule that said that a monster has to shut up when it is told to.'

'I'm always quiet and dignified,' said the monster. 'Why would anyone want me to shut up?'

'Yeah right and you—' began Moin.

'Moin, who are you talking to?' asked Colander. She had been sent to fetch him.

MONSTER RULE 222

A monster does not belong to the human with whom it stays.

'Are you nervous? I do that, you know. I start talking to myself when I get nervous. That really helps. I tell myself stories and sometimes I sing songs. It calms me down.'

'Me too,' said the monster.

Colander looked at Moin in alarm. 'What happened to your voice? You sound weird. Do you have a sore throat? How will you sing?'

'There's nothing—' began the monster, but Moin clamped its mouth shut. He cleared his throat.

'I was just clearing my throat. For the performance, you know,' he said.

'Oh the gargling exercise? I did that yesterday, and my voice really cleared up.

Come, there's no time for it now. See, the curtain's about to go up.'

Moin put the monster in his pocket. Fortunately, it was a button-down pocket. He made sure the button was properly fastened, and ignoring the thumping and the muffled 'urghs' of the monster, he followed Colander to the stage.

In the auditorium, Moin's father, Mr Kaif, was trying to find the most inconspicuous seat, as close to the door as possible.

Moin's mother understood the feeling, but she felt it would be unfair to Moin. 'He might look for us, and he'll be so disappointed if he can't see us,' she said.

'Oh okay,' said Mr Kaif, and put on his glasses.

'How can you see properly in those? It's so dark,' said Mrs Kaif.

Mr Kaif couldn't see anything. There were some blurred dark things about, and he could barely make out if they were things or people. But he was not going to admit it. So he stretched his hands out and groped his way towards what he felt was the most remote corner of the auditorium.

'Ow!' he yelled, stubbing his toe against a hard object. It could have been the foot of a chair or even someone's shoe. He couldn't see.

One of the young volunteers, who was helping people find seats, came running. She saw a man in a hat and dark glasses groping about and tripping.

'Oh no,' she said, because she was a soft-hearted soul. 'Here. Let me help you, uncle.' She took his hand and led him to the front row. 'You'll be able to hear properly from here,' she said sweetly as she sat him down right in the middle of the first row.

A moment later, his wife joined him. 'Well done!' she said bitterly. 'Very inconspicuous.'

'No one will recognise me,' said Mr Kaif, hopefully. 'In fact, you should cover your head with your dupatta. Then no one will know who we are.'

Since Tony's parents had to leave early they were sitting somewhere at the back. But Parvati's parents were sitting right behind them. Moin's father couldn't see them because of the glasses, but his mother had already smiled and greeted them.

'Hey Kaif!' Parvati's father called out, dashing Mr Kaif's hopes of anonymity. 'Looking very dashing in the hat and goggles, boss!'

Mr Kaif took off his glasses and laughed weakly.

'Excuse me, sir,' said a little old lady sitting right behind him. 'If you don't mind, can you take off that hat, please? I can't see the stage.'

Mr Kaif took off his hat. Feeling naked and vulnerable, he waited for the curtain to rise.

CURTAINS UP

There was a sigh of relief in the audience when the curtain rose.

Tothogotho Chowdhury stood centrestage, beaming at the audience of doting mothers, proud fathers, fond grandparents, critical aunts, grumpy uncles and reluctant cousins. There was also the odd teacher and, as it happened, a very odd principal.

Kooki had recovered from the shock of seeing the pink apparition. With great patience, Dr Reddy had convinced him that the pink thing he had seen was a figment of his imagination.

'Did you see it?' he asked Mrs Kooki.

'I did not,' answered Mrs Kooki. She had made her peace with Dr Reddy, and had even given him an aspirin for the headache her knock on the head had given him.

'Neither did I,' said Dr Reddy.

'But … but … but those children were running behind it, and they were the same children!' said Kooki.

'Same as what, Sir?' asked his wife.

Kooki had to give his wife a quick explanation of how he knew Dr Reddy. 'And when that pink thing came and sang in my office these three children turned up suddenly and said they couldn't hear anything, and the pink thing I saw turned out to be a drawing done by the Boeing boy,' he concluded.

'What happened is that you associated the appearance of the pink thing with these three children, so it is a clear case of Associative Suggestion leading to Acute Cognitive Hallucination,' said Dr Reddy, very excited. This case was one of the most interesting ones of his career. In fact, it was only the second case of AS-induced ACH that had come to him, and the first one was an alcoholic, so it didn't count.

He took out his phone and quickly made a note of it.

'Huh?' asked Kooki.

'I think we should go in and sit down, Sir,' said Mrs Kooki firmly. 'The music will soothe your nerves.'

Kooki doubted if the singing would do anything except irritate his nerves, but he knew there was no point arguing.

So they went into the auditorium and found seats in the front row, a few seats away from Mr and Mrs Kaif.

Tothogotho had, meanwhile, finished welcoming everyone and garlanding the chief guest, who held some important government post somewhere in the hills.

'He has come all the way from the mountains to grace this occasion. So please give him a big hand!' he said.

'He must be mad,' muttered Mr Kaif. 'If he had any sense he'd have headed higher into the hills.'

'Oh dear,' said Mrs Kaif, very worried. Moin was going to sing in front of important government officials! She wished now that she had pretended to have a headache. Maybe she could still do it.

But before she could say anything, Tothogotho announced, 'Let me introduce our first singer, one of my most talented students, Moin Kaif!'

There was loud applause from the parts of the audience where Moin was known. The others clapped weakly, as if to say, okay, so get on with it.

Moin came on stage, looking nervous.

'Oh poor thing!' said Mrs Kaif. 'He's scared. See how he's holding his pounding heart.'

Actually, it was Moin's pocket that was pounding. The monster was hopping up and down in excitement at being on stage.

'He's an idiot!' hissed Parvati to Tony. 'He's taken it on stage. Now there's no stopping it.'

The musicians started playing the tune. The audience waited to hear Tothogotho's most talented student.

Moin opened his mouth to sing.

What shrieked out of the loudspeakers was a voice like no one had heard before:

If you're in a pocket
All buttoned up and tight,
Then you have to sing a song
Loud, with all your might.

Sing-a sing-a sing-a
A song-a bong-a bing-a
Sing-a sing-a sing-a
A song-a bongaling!

The musicians stopped playing in shock.

Moin was trying to move his mouth to the

monster's words so that people would think he
was singing.

Tothogotho stood with his mouth open.
Moin's parents were sobbing openly.
And still the song went on:

It's not easy to sing-a
Sitting in a pocket,
But if you want to swing-a
Then you will have to rock it.

Oh sing-a sing-a sing-a
A song-a bong-a bing-a

Sing-a sing-a sing-a
A song-a bongaling!

A pocket is a docket
But if it's on a stage,
You only have to sing-a
And you'll be all the rage.

The audience exploded in delight. Many of them had come because they had to, dreading the thought of sitting through an evening of dull classical music. The children, especially, were joyous. They stood in the seats and danced, wiggling their hips, clapping and singing along:

Sing-a sing-a sing-a
A song-a bong-a bing-a
Sing-a sing-a sing-a
A song-a bongaling!

The monster had managed to prise Moin's pocket open enough to peer at the audience, and it was pleased as punch. It would not stop singing. Moin was too busy trying to lip-sync to think clearly, but Tony and Parvati realised that this could go on forever. They ran up to the stage, grabbed Moin and pushed him off stage.

The audience booed and yelled 'ENCORE!'.

The rest of the concert was a complete disaster. Every time someone started an alaap or a kirtan, the children started chanting 'We want Mo-in! We want Mo-in!'

But Moin's parents had taken him home. They grounded him for two weeks.

'And no singing for a month!' said Mr Kaif, seeing an opportunity.

Mrs Kaif looked at him in admiration. 'What a good idea!' she said.

COLOUR WASH

'How long will it last?' asked Tony.

'How long will what last?'

'The no-singing rule. Forever? So the monster will never be allowed to sing again?'

'WHAT?' yelled the monster, from the cupboard. 'I'll never be allowed to sing again? How can you do that? You can't repress my creativity! You can't suppress my talent! It's against the rules!'

Tony got very excited. 'Is there a rule about that? Can you remember the rule?' he asked. He was about to unlock the cupboard to let the monster out, so he could write down the rule in his book.

'No!' yelled Moin. 'We'll let you out if you promise not to sing.'

'I can't make such rash promises,' said the monster.

'Come on,' called Tony. 'You know Moin will get into trouble if you sing. You have to follow his parents' rules here. They're just like your monster rules. They can't be disobeyed.'

'I can sing softly. His parents won't hear. I can promise not to sing loudly.'

Tony waggled his eyebrows at Moin.

'Oh okay,' said Moin. 'But you have to stop when I tell you to.'

'Only if there's a good reason.'

Moin scowled. 'That's reasonable,' said Tony.

Moin was not at all happy.

He knew that what was a good reason to him may not be a good reason to the monster. On the other hand, he couldn't keep the monster locked up for the whole month, which was how long he'd been banned from singing. It liked lolling around in there, but Moin would need to take out his clothes and things from the cupboard from time to time. Besides, he'd have to feed the monster. He didn't want it eating bananas and dates in the cupboard. It would chuck the peels and seeds among his clothes and they would stink.

So he decided that making a deal was the best thing to do.

'Okay,' he said and opened the cupboard. The monster grinned at him.

'What's the rule?' asked Tony.

'Something about not being able to change the nature of a monster. I can't remember the exact words.'

'I told you!' said Moin. 'I told you it makes up rules.'

'I don't! I just can't remember properly. I'll tell you when I remember,' the monster told a disappointed Tony.

The monster hopped out of the cupboard and hopped on to the window sill, which was its second favourite place in the room, after the cupboard.

'So let's do the purple,' it said.

Moin thought it was a very bad idea, but he took out his new crayons, anyway.

'Get flat,' he told the monster. The monster turned into a flat piece of paper, and Tony and Moin tried to turn it from pink to purple.

It was useless. They rubbed and pressed till the monster squeaked, but the colour just wouldn't stick.

'Bah,' said the monster, turning into itself again. 'I have to stay this horrible pink forever.'

'Maybe it will wash off,' Tony said. He was always curious and ready to experiment.

Moin scowled at him. 'Stop giving it ideas.

It's not going to wash off. So forget that,' he said to the monster.

But the monster did not forget it.

The next day, when Moin's father picked up Moin's clothes to dump into the laundry basket, the monster flattened itself and slipped into the folds of Moin's shirt.

It was warm and comfortable in the basket, but the monster was unhappy with the smells. It could smell some orange juice that Moin had spilt on his shirt the previous day. It smelt sour and stale. It could also smell egg and a mix of masalas. Probably from the hand towel that had lodged itself near its ear. It decided to stay still, though, because it wanted to try out Tony's idea, and it knew that if Moin found it, he would drag it out at once.

Moin was going quite frantic, meanwhile. It was time to go to school, and he needed to make sure the monster was safely in the room before he locked it up. But he couldn't find it anywhere. He had turned his room upside down: clothes were pulled out of the cupboard, the bed linen was yanked off, in case it was hiding in there, and even his books were taken off the shelf and given a good shake. But the monster seemed to have disappeared.

After checking his bag to make sure that it hadn't sneaked in, Moin left.

'Maybe it's gone!' Parvati said, when Moin told her and Tony about it.

'Oh no!' said Tony.

'No such luck,' said Moin mournfully. 'It'll do something stupid and I'll get into trouble.'

'You have to find a way to get rid of it,' said Parvati. 'I'll think of something.'

Moin sighed. He didn't have much hope.

The monster was singing sleepily in the laundry basket. Because it had promised, it was singing in a sort of hoarse whisper:

Oh oh oh
What a stink!
But I'll do anything I can
To be rid of the pink!

No no no
No more pink!
I'll get a proper washing
And be unpinked in a wink.

Moin's mother came to pick up the washing and heard a strange buzzing sound in the basket. She thought there might be a bee in it and took out the clothes very carefully. But no bee flew out.

'Hmm,' she frowned. But she had no time to investigate. 'The buzzing must have come from outside,' she told herself. She quickly dumped the clothes into the washing machine, switched it on and left for work.

While Moin worried himself sick at school and his mother kept popping her ears, in case the buzzing was inside them, the monster went round and round in the washing machine with the clothes.

Strangely enough, the monster didn't drown. Neither the water nor the spinning bothered it.

MONSTER RULE II

Monsters don't need to breathe like humans.

'Wheeeeeee!' it yelled.

Round and round and round I go
Round and round and round I go
Round and round and round I go
Round and round I go, whee!

The pinky pink will go I know
The pinky pink will go I know
The pinky pink will go I know
The pinky pink will go, whee!

It sang this loudly, but that was okay, because the whirring of the machine drowned its voice and anyway, there was no one around to hear it.

An hour later, when Myna, the girl who came to clean up, took the clothes out of the machine to hang them up to dry, she started at the sight of the paper in the machine.

'That Moin!' she thought to herself. 'So careless. What if all the clothes had become coloured?'

She hung the monster on the line along with the clothes, clipping it in place with a clothespin. The monster didn't mind the clothespin or even being hung upside down.

But to its disgust and disappointment, it was still pink.

KOOKI PAYS A VISIT

Principal K.K. Kuttykrishnan was not in his office. In fact, he was not even in school.

He was still recovering from his evening at the concert. When Moin went on stage and the song began, Kooki froze. His eyes popped and looked as if they might fall on his lap.

'Guggugugugugggg …' he said, pointing at the stage. Mrs Kooki had to take him home.

'It was just a boy singing badly, Sir,' Mrs Kooki told him on their way back. 'I know, it is very surprising that Tothogothoji thinks he's a brilliant singer and all, but we all make mistakes.'

'Guguguuguug …' said Kooki.

'He must be having a soft spot for the boy. Such a sweet boy. Very odd it was, to hear his voice. But you must not get so upset, Sir.'

It took two filter coffees and a whole packet of banana chips to unlock Kooki's voice.

'It was that thing!' he said when the last sip of coffee had trickled through his throat.

Mrs Kooki clucked. Kooki seemed to be getting more inarticulate by the day.

'Which was what thing?' she asked, not letting her impatience show. She was a very good teacher.

'Teacher, remember I told you about that pink thing that sang in my office, enh? It was the exact same voice, Teacher! Exactly, precisely the same.'

Mrs Kooki wanted to point out that exactly and precisely meant the same thing and one of the words was unnecessary, but she wisely realised that this was not the time to dwell on language.

'Maybe it was the boy singing in your office,' she suggested.

But Kooki insisted that the boy was not there when the singing happened. Mrs Kooki wanted to tell him he was imagining it all, but Kooki seemed very agitated. She didn't want to distress him any more. He was even convinced that there had been something pink sticking out of Moin's pocket.

'And the voice was coming from there,

Teacher, from his pocket! I am sure, I am sure of it!'

'He could have had a pink handkerchief, Sir,' was Mrs Kooki's sensible reply.

But Kooki refused to be soothed by sense.

Finally, Mrs Kooki set up another appointment for Kooki with Dr Reddy. So while Moin fretted, his mother popped her ears and the monster went round and round in the washing machine, Kooki was talking to Dr Reddy.

'You seem to have a lot of hostility in you towards this child,' Dr Reddy told him after three hours during which Kooki relived the singing in his office, the pink creature running in the auditorium and the glimpse of pink when Moin sang. Dr Reddy encouraged him gently to talk, and took furious notes. After Kooki had talked for a long time, Dr Reddy felt he could finally stop listening and give his opinion.

'I have no hostility towards Boeing,' Kooki said.

'That is a classic case of denial,' said Dr Reddy.

'Anh, I am denying it,' agreed Kooki.

'Our mind plays subtle tricks on us so we think we are agreeing with something, when actually we are resisting it. So you accept

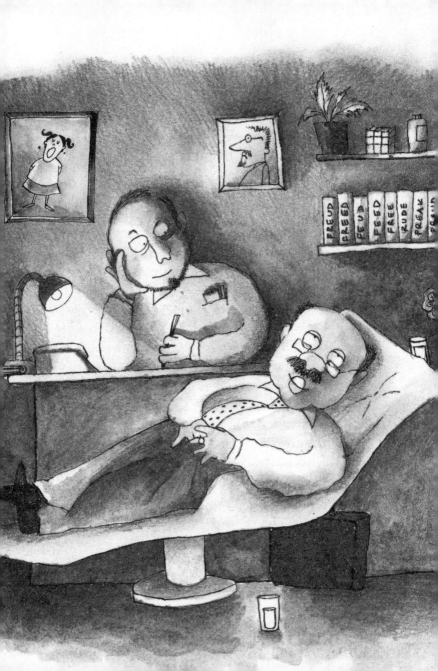

your denial but in fact you are resisting my suggestion that you are in denial.'

Kooki's brain began a slow spin.

'So you see,' Dr Reddy continued, 'the only way to stop this cycle of acceptance and denial is by colliding with the premise in a direct and sympathetic manner.'

Kooki's brain began to spin so fast he could almost hear it hum.

'Colliding with a premise?' he heard himself say in a dazed way. 'What does that mean? Is it possible to collide with a premise, enh?'

'In practical terms, Mr Kuttykrishnan,' said Dr Reddy, in the gentle voice which he had practiced for years, in order not to excite his more excitable patients, 'what you should do is try and get to know this boy, so that your resentment and anger is dimmed. You will feel at peace.'

Kooki sighed. He didn't agree, but not to agree was to deny, and this, it seemed was a sign of his illness.

'What should I do, enh?' he asked resignedly.

'Why don't you go and pay this boy a visit? Go to his house, see him outside school, make friends with him and his parents … You need to get rid of the hostile and negative feelings that you associate with the boy. Then you'll stop seeing strange things and hearing voices. Though I must agree that he sings very badly.'

Dr Reddy's daughter, Colander (which was not her real name, of course), had not been allowed to sing by the heckling crowd who wanted Moin back after he sang at the concert. Dr Reddy shook his head and told himself he ought to be above petty thoughts.

'Go meet the boy, sir,' he said calmly, trying not to remember his daughter's howling at having her performance ruined. It had taken a lot of ice cream and a promised trip to Disneyland to stop her tantrum.

So that afternoon, while Moin headed towards his house after school, Kooki headed towards Moin's house.

Moin's mother opened the door, and her first thought was that something horrible had happened to Moin. Her second thought was that Moin had finally done something so horrible that the principal had to come personally to inform them.

But Kooki was smiling his friendliest smile. It was a bit scary, because Moin's mother could see his gums right up to the point where they met his jaws, but he was definitely smiling.

'Good evening, Mrs Kaif,' said Kooki. 'You are surprised to see me, anh?'

Mrs Kaif realised that her mouth was still hanging open. She shut it quickly.

'Um, yes,' she said. 'What a pleasant surprise! Please come in.'

Kooki went in and sat down. There was a long and uncomfortable silence. Mrs Kaif didn't want to ask him 'Why are you here?' because it sounded rude, but she couldn't think of anything else to ask or say.

So she waited for Kooki to speak. But Kooki was thinking longingly about his evening coffee, and didn't say anything for a long time.

Suddenly, he looked up and saw Mrs Kaif staring at him. He cleared his throat.

'Isn't ...' he was about to say Boeing, but somehow, just in time, it occurred to him that that could not be the boy's name. He spluttered, coughed and started again: 'Isn't your son home from school?'

Mrs Kaif smiled in relief. 'In about five minutes,' she said. 'The bus takes a slightly long route. Have you come straight from school?'

'No, no,' said Kooki.

Silence.

If Mrs Kaif waited for an explanation of why Kooki had not come straight from school, she waited in vain. Kooki was thinking of a cup of delicious, fragrant filter coffee. He was beginning to wish he had not given in to the impulse to come straight here instead of going home first.

More silence.

Mrs Kaif's feet began to sweat. The stress was getting to her. Another moment and she would start hiccuping. Stress did that to her. She got up quickly.

'Let me get you something to drink? Tea? Coffee?'

'Coffee!' Kooki almost shouted.

Looking a bit surprised, Mrs Kaif went into the kitchen to make coffee. Since they rarely drank coffee, she had to search for the instant coffee. When she found it, she saw that the coffee had become a solid mass and was stuck to the jar. She took a fork and began to dig at it, and managed to get a few flakes, but it wouldn't be enough. The only way to get it out would be to heat some water and pour it in and use that as a sort of concentrated decoction.

Kooki was getting restless. The coffee seemed to be a long time coming. He got up and wandered around, looking at pictures of Moin smiling, frowning and making funny faces at the camera. He wondered why parents always wanted so many pictures of their

children around. Wasn't it enough that *they* were always around?

Then he wandered out on to the balcony. On one side, there were a few chairs and a low table and potted plants. The other side was a sort of work area, with a clothesline and an ironing table.

Kooki glanced at the clothesline and froze.

Mrs Kaif, coming in with the coffee, saw Kooki standing on the balcony.

'Here you are,' she said brightly, going up to him.

'Gugugugugugug,' said Kooki, pointing at the monster on the clothesline.

THE RIGHT QUESTION

'It's simple,' said Parvati. 'Ask the right question and you'll get the right answer.'

Tony didn't agree. He'd been asking the monster all kinds of questions, but all he ever got in response were some monster rules, some really bad songs and sometimes, if he used big words, a snore.

Moin, Parvati and Tony had examined the monster rules and read *The Strange Behaviour of Monsters* over and over, but there wasn't a single clue to where it had come from, and more importantly, how they could send it back.

Moin had got into trouble again, for putting his 'drawing' into the washing machine. 'It's all your fault,' he told Tony. 'You gave it the idea. So now you have to help me.'

'I still think it might be an alien,' said Tony.

But their attempt to prove that theory had ended in disaster and a broken telescope.

'I'm sure there's some way of finding out. Maybe we should get a brain surgeon to examine its brain,' said Tony.

'It doesn't *have* a brain,' said Moin bitterly.

'Okay,' said Parvati taking charge, 'let's make a list of questions that we can ask.' They were all in Parvati's house and she had a whiteboard in her room. Moin was sitting on the floor and Tony was at the desk, decorating the cover of his *Monster Rule Book* with bright coloured cellotape.

Parvati drew a diagram on her whiteboard as she spoke.

'So here's the monster, and this is Moin. And this is—'

'That's not like me at all. I don't have such a big head,' said Moin.

'It's exactly like you,' Parvati said.

'I don't have sticking-out ears,' Moin pointed out. 'And anyway, I don't see why I have to be there in the diagram. It could be anyone. That's not got anything to do with anything.'

'HEY!' yelled Tony.

Parvati dropped her marker in alarm, and it fell on her foot.

'Ow!' she shouted, hopping up and down on one leg. 'Why'd you do that?'

'Wait! Listen! I know what!' said Tony.

Parvati hit him on the head with a cushion and satisfied that she'd got her revenge, she sat down. 'What?'

'I know the right question to ask. It's not where it came from but why. Why did it come?'

'Some stupid monster rule,' said Moin.

'No, but really, why is it here? Let's ask it. Maybe it has a task of some kind, so when it finishes the task it'll go.'

'What kind of task?' asked Parvati.

'I don't know … we'll have to think. What could it be?'

There was a minute of silence while Moin, Parvati and Tony thought of the monster.

'To finish off all the bananas in the world,' said Moin.

'To make everyone deaf with its horrible singing,' said Parvati.

'To cover the floor of my room with date seeds.'

Tony sighed. 'I'll ask it,' he said. 'It talks to me.'

But when they asked the monster the following day, it said it didn't know what a task was.

'It's something you have to do,' Tony explained.

'Like a rule?' asked the monster.

'No, not like a rule, but like a ... like work. Like something you have to finish.'

'Sounds stupid,' said the monster. 'Hey! This banana is not squishy enough!'

'Doesn't anyone do any work in the monster world?' asked Parvati.

'Nope. Against the rules,' said the monster through a mouthful of banana.

'You really think there can be a rule like that? I'm telling you, it's making these rules up. How can people not work?'

'I'm not people,' said the monster.

MONSTER RULE 197

There's no such thing as work.

'That's true,' said Tony. 'So if monsters don't work, what do you do?'

'I sing. I dance. I eat bananas.'

'That's here,' said Tony. 'But what do you do in the monster world? Do you eat bananas there? Where are they grown? Who grows them?'

'Ouch!' yelled the monster. 'Don't ask so many questions. It gives me a stomach ache.'

'That's the bananas, not the questions,' Moin informed it.

'Bananas are good for me.'

'So, do you have them in the monster world?' asked Tony again.

'What's a monster world?' asked the monster. It had discovered that it could push a date seed through one nostril and pull it out through the other, and it was busy perfecting this very rare art.

'Who makes the monster rules?' Moin asked.

'Stop asking me all these questions. You're making my stomach ache,' said the monster.

'I think there's only one thing to do,' said Parvati.

'What?' asked Moin. He was prepared to do anything if it meant he could go back to being monsterless again.

'Learn to live with it,' said Parvati.

Moin groaned.

A LOOPY REQUEST

'No one's saying anything,' whispered Parvati.

Moin and she were hiding behind a chest of drawers just outside the door of the drawing room. Tony was hiding under a low table on the other side, but he didn't quite fit. Parts of him were sticking out on all sides.

Tothogotho Chowdhury had called to say he wanted to see Moin's parents. Moin had been told to stay out of the way, because his parents didn't think Tothogotho would want to see him after the way he had ruined the concert.

But Parvati and Tony had come over, and the three children decided to eavesdrop. Except there was nothing to eavesdrop on, because everyone was silent.

Mr and Mrs Kaif were silent because the

great man's concert had been a complete
tamasha, and they knew it was all their son's
fault. So after the initial greeting, they sat
silent, like people at a funeral who didn't know
what to say.

Tothogotho was silent because what he
had come to say stuck in his throat. It was
embarrassing and infuriating, and he had
been forced to come to talk to Moin's parents
against his will.

'I hope you won't stand in the way of the
boy's fame just because you don't agree with
the genre,' his brother-in-law had told him.

'Genre!' Tothogotho had muttered to
himself. 'As if people screaming to the banging
of pots and pans is a musical genre!'

Very few people knew this, but Tothogotho

Chowdhury was married to the sister of the world-famous composer Loopy Bagiri. His real name was L. Upender Bagiri, but everyone called him Loopy. Chowdury detested him and his music, but he could never admit that aloud. His wife adored her little brother (if someone who weighed a hundred and fifty kilos could be called little) and would put Tothogotho on a diet of bitter-gourd juice forever if he even hinted at his disapproval. She was always threatening this.

Loopy Bagiri composed a good song every now and then, but Tothogotho could not forgive the bad ones. One of them sounded like a train was running on a defective track, while thousands of people shrieked tonelessly from inside it. Another sounded like donkeys braying while horses galloped on a tin roof.

And to make matters worse, there was Loopy himself. He had been told by an astrologer that he should always wear yellow.

'So that you will shine like the sun in your life!' the astrologer had said.

So Loopy wore a yellow shirt, yellow trousers, and yellow socks. His shoes were usually black, though he wore white shoes for special occasions, with a white tie. As if this wasn't bad enough, he wore gold-rimmed goggles, a hideous gold watch and what looked

like hundreds of gold chains around his neck. They actually clanged when he walked.

When Loopy said he wanted to meet 'that boy Moin, who sang the brilliant song at the concert', Tothogotho was very upset. He had barely got over the shock of hearing his star singer shrieking like a seagull. And what was that song he had been singing? It was an outrage!

And here was Loopy praising him and wanting to meet him. But Tothogotho's wife was looking at him with narrowed eyes, that said 'bitter-gourd juice' in capital letters, so he sniffed and said, 'I'll give you the address.'

Unfortunately, Loopy was going off on a world tour with his band. Tothogotho could never understand why anyone anywhere in the world would want to hear Loopy's music, but there it was. People actually paid him huge amounts of money to shriek into their ears. And when he came back he was going to hold a massive musical concert, and he wanted Moin to sing at it. He was going to compose a special song just for Moin.

'The boy is a star! That voice! Those lyrics! Did you see how the crowd went wild for him? I must have him for my concert. I have no time to go meet his parents, Tutudada,' he said. 'You'll have to do it for me.'

So it was no wonder Tothogotho was tongue-tied.

'Ahem,' he said at last. Though that was not so much saying as doing.

Mrs Kaif gave Tothogotho a glass of water.

Outside, Parvati whispered, 'Ahem? What does that even mean?'

Inside, Tothogotho continued. 'I've actually come on behalf of Loopy Bagiri.'

By the time he'd explained Loopy's request, Moin's parents didn't know whether to laugh or cry.

'We'll need to think about it,' Mrs Kaif said, wondering how to say no.

'He needs to focus on his studies,' said Mr Kaif. The thought of enduring another evening lurking in dark corners with a hat and goggles did not appeal to him at all.

'Good decision!' said Tothogotho and left quickly before they could change their minds.

Mr and Mrs Kaif did a high five in relief.

Tothogotho went away, humming the alaap of his favourite raaga.

Moin, Parvati and Tony giggled at what they'd heard, in Moin's room. Everyone was pleased with the way the visit had turned out.

Except the monster.

'Hey!' it said. 'I want to sing in the concert. He wants me, not you! So you have no right to say no.'

'I didn't say no, my parents did,' Moin pointed out.

'They're not my parents. They can't decide for me. There's a monster rule.'

MONSTER RULE 404

Human parents cannot take decisions for monsters

'Who's going to tell them that?' asked Moin.

'You!' said the monster.

'No way,' said Moin.

But the monser knew how to get its way. It started yodelling.

Yodelly-yoo-yodelly-yoo!
Woo-hoooo-hooo!

Parvati and Tony suddenly remembered they needed to go home.

'Stop!' yelled Moin. Just in time, because Moin's mother and father had come running.

'What is it? Are you hurt? We heard you howling!' they said.

Moin grabbed the chance.

'I'm not howling. Only sort of moaning. I have this urge to sing, but I'm not allowed to sing, so I moan. Wooo-hoo-hooooo.'

'Oh,' said Moin's father.

Moin's mother wiped a tear from her eye. 'We're depriving him of an opportunity, you know,' she said to Mr Kaif as they went back to the drawing room. They had been talking about the concert and whether they had done the right thing by saying no to Loopy.

'I think they might change their minds,' Moin said to the monster.

'You'll have to keep at them,' said the monster.

'You're always making me do things and you never do anything. You don't even answer our questions. I don't know why I should bother.'

'If you let me sing for Loopy Bagiri, I'll tell you where I came from,' said the monster.

'Promise?'

'I don't need to promise. I can't lie. Rule,'

said the monster as it settled down to finish a
bowl of bananas.

MONSTER RULE 83

Monsters cannot lie.

'Bah,' said Moin. 'I bet that's a lie.'

MONSTER SONGSTER

Parvati, Tony and Moin were sitting in Loopy Bagiri's office. The monster was in Moin's pocket.

When Moin had asked his parents if he, Parvati and Tony could go by themselves, his father had said, 'Yes!'

'No need to shout so loudly,' Moin had said, frowning.

'How nice for you to go with your friends,' his mother had said. He thought she sounded a little breathless. Moin thought he heard the two of them giggling when he left the room, but he couldn't be sure.

Tony's father dropped the three of them off at Loopy Bagiri's office and Parvati's mother would pick them up later and take them to Parvati's house.

'You'd better behave yourself,' Moin said to his pocket.

'You sound like a mommy,' said his pocket rudely.

'I should have never listened to it,' Moin told Parvati and Tony. 'I bet we're going to get into all kinds of trouble.'

'I told you it was a bad idea,' said Parvati.

'It'll be fine,' said Tony. 'And we'll get some important information, which might help us in our future strategies.'

'Ha,' said Moin. Then he said, 'Yaaa!' because his pocket had started humming.

'Stop it!' Moin said.

'You didn't let me practise,' said his pocket.

'Of course I did. You were singing in the bathroom for three hours yesterday. I nearly went deaf.'

'That's not enough. We artistes need to practise for hours and hours and hours. You won't understand.'

'It's not like you'll get any better,' said Parvati rudely.

'This is true,' said the monster. 'I'm already perfect.'

'Perfectly rotten,' muttered Moin. But the monster heard him and began to hum even louder.

If you call me rotten
You will start to rot
Because whatever's rotten
Will rot whatever's not!

it sang.

'SHHHH!' said Parvati, Moin and Tony, all together.

Just at that moment, Loopy Bagiri walked in. The children gasped.

Not because they were impressed with Loopy, but because Loopy drifted in on a cloud of the strongest perfume. He was in his glorious yellow best.

'He looks like a giant sunflower,' Parvati whispered to Tony.

'Aha! So here is the genius singer!' said Loopy, putting a fat arm around Moin. Moin nearly gagged. Later, he swore that his brain died for a second, but Tony told him that was impossible. Brains couldn't die from smell.

Loopy's voice was strangely hoarse and low. It made everything he said sound somehow secretive and sinister.

'Where did you learn to sing like that?' Loopy continued. 'Not at Chowdhury's! He only teaches boring classical stuff! You and I know how to rock, eh, Genius? You know what? I think I'll change your name! What's your current name?'

'Current name?' asked Moin, imagining electric current going through a nameplate.

'He means what's your name now. Current as in present, not current as in electricity,' Tony explained. He knew how Moin's mind worked.

'My name now? It's the same as before. My name doesn't keep changing. It's Moin Kaif.'

'Moin Kaif! Mo-in Ka-if! Nope! No way! Too tame! What about Mean Machine? Cool huh? Moin the Mean Machine! You don't look too happy with that! Too angry? What about Ba-ba Sheep? It has a certain ring to it!'

'No!' yelled a voice from Moin's pocket. 'I will not—'

'NO!' yelled Parvati at once, trying to drown the monster's voice. 'WHAT ABOUT MONSTER SONGSTER?' It was the first thing that came to her head.

The effect on Loopy was electric (as in current). 'LITTLE GIRL!' he shrieked, 'You are a GENIUS! Are all your friends geniuses, boy? Monster Songster! What rhyming! What image! What a perfect name! Monster Songster! Monster Songster! Monster Songster! Monster Songster!'

He would have said it a few times more if his assistant had not come to say that the musicians were waiting to start the recording.

In the chaos of Loopy's yelling and being herded inside, no one except Tony heard the monster say, 'That is a tautology.'

'You mean all monsters are songsters?' asked Tony, thinking this was an important clue to the monster's origins.

'Yup!' said the monster. 'It's so obvious it's not even a rule.'

Then Moin was whisked away by Loopy and Tony couldn't speak to his pocket any more.

Loopy took Moin to his musicians and shouted, 'Meet Moin the Monster Songster! Nice name, huh? Huh? Monster Songster! Heh heh! Heh heh! Heh heh heh!' He cackled for five minutes while his musicians looked on impatiently.

'Can we hear the boy's song now?' asked the violinist, when Loopy had stopped laughing.

'The boy! The song! So Monster Songster, what song are you singing for us?'

'Um, can I just sing it?' asked Moin. The monster had refused to prepare or give Moin any idea of what it would sing.

'I'm spontaneous,' it had said. 'The song I practise may not be the song I sing.' Moin hoped not, because he was sick of hearing the song that the monster practised. Besides, it was awful.

Moin went to the microphone with a heavy feeling in his stomach. It was either the French fries that he had eaten at tea time or fear. He would have to pretend to sing a song that he had never heard before. Again.

'One … two … three … go!' said Loopy Bagiri.

Yellow man!
Yellow man!
What a dirty fellow, man!

Can he sing a song
Does he even know to sing?
Why does yellow fellow
Have so many chains and rings?
He glints like gold because
He's hung with lots of golden things!
I've never seen a fellow, man
With such a lot of bling!

Yeah!

Yellow man!
Yellow man!
What a dirty fellow,
Man!

Yellow man!
Yellow man!
Sounds like a buffalo, man!

Yellow man!
Yellow man!
Yellow fellow man!

When the monster stopped singing, Moin gulped. Parvati was standing with her hands across her mouth, and her eyes almost popping out of her head. Tony had chosen a dark spot under the table and sat there, with his head on his knees.

Moin looked at Loopy.

Loopy was grinning. 'Ha ha! A song about me! Very flattering! I thought I would write a special song for you, but this is much better! A protégé writing a song for his mentor! Very good! Very good!!'

Moin had no idea what he was on about. Was he calling Moin a prodigy? Was he calling himself mental? He must be mental, if he liked the rude song the monster had made up about him.

'Just some changes in the words! And one or two changes in the tune! Right?'

A few minutes later, Moin was back at the microphone with a new set of words:

Yellow man!
Yellow man!
What a super fellow, man!

He's a first-class singer
He is awesome when he sings

How handsome yellow fellow looks
With all his chains and rings!
He's good as gold and that is why
He wears those golden things!

Yeah!

Yellow man!
Yellow man!
What a splendid fellow,
Man!

Yellow man!
Yellow man!
Awesome, super, splendid, first-class
Yellow fellow man!

But the monster refused to sing the new
words.

'I cannot compromise my art,' it said. It
wouldn't listen to Moin. Moin pretended to go
to the loo and Tony and Parvati tried to talk to
the monster.

'It's just a few words. You can do it,' said
Tony.

'Will not,' said the monster.

'No more bananas, then,' said Parvati
sternly.

'Okay,' said the monster. 'I don't have to eat. I just like to eat.'

MONSTER RULE 5

Monsters can survive without eating in the human world.

'What?!' shouted Moin, remembering all the times he'd had to smuggle bananas and dates for the monster.

'Actually,' said Tony, 'if it doesn't want to sing, how does it matter?'

'Matter? What am I going to tell my parents after all the fuss I made to get them to agree? That I suddenly didn't feel like singing? You have to sing!' Moin told the monster again.

'If you want to sing that terrible song, you sing it. I won't,' said the monster.

Parvati and Tony looked at each other.

'Of course! Why didn't we think of that!' said Parvati.

SWEET

'Too sweet?' Mrs Kaif repeated for the fourth time, looking dazed.

They had had a call from Loopy Bagiri. 'I'm not at all happy with Moin's singing,' he told Moin's mother.

'What happened?' asked Mrs Kaif. 'Does that mean he won't be singing at the concert?'

Mr Kaif looked up hopefully from the ground, where he had collapsed halfway through his sit-ups.

'Not at all happy, madam!' Loopy continued. 'When I heard him at Tothogotho Chowdhury's concert, what a fresh powerful voice he had! What a song he sang!'

Loopy broke into song in his famous hoarse voice:

Sing-a sing-a sing-a
A song-a bong-a bing-a
Sing-a sing-a sing-a
A song-a bongaling!

Mrs Kaif wished she had stuffed her ears with cotton. She had hoped never to hear that song again, and definitely not in a voice like Loopy's. 'Yes, yes,' she mumbled into the phone.

'But now, something has gone wrong. His voice has become too sweet!'

'Too s-sweet?' Mrs Kaif repeated faintly. 'Really?'

'First, he sang well, but I had to change the words and the tune a little, and after that, it was all downhill! No attitude, no emotion! You

know my work, Mrs Kaif. It's all about depth and emotion.'

The only song of Loopy's that Mrs Kaif had heard went:

Chum chumachum choo choo choo

Dum dumadum doo doo doo

The words were repeated over and over, in a thin and high and wailing voice. Mrs Kaif had felt like the song was making a deep hole inside her head, and she had felt a strong emotional urge to cut off her ears. She wondered if that's what he meant by depth and emotion.

'Of course, of course,' she said on the phone. 'I understand if you can't have him in your concert.'

Mr Kaif sat up, beaming with hope.

'No, no, I want him!' Loopy cried. 'He is a musical genius. But I will send a special medicine for him. It's a magic potion, madam! That's what I drink every day! Very soon, your son will become the next Loopy Bagiri!'

'Oh no,' said Mrs Kaif. Fortunately, Loopy had disconnected.

'He says Moin's voice is too sweet. Too sweet? Too sweet?'

'So does that mean he won't sing at the concert?' Mr Kaif asked, getting up and preparing to dance a jig.

'You wish,' said Mrs Kaif bitterly.

Back at Parvati's house, Parvati and Tony were rolling on the floor, laughing like hyenas. The monster was swinging from the curtains, singing softly to itself.

'Did you see Loopy's face when Moin started singing?' Parvati asked Tony. 'It was like a comic.'

'It was a great idea to get Moin to sing like the monster.'

'It was a rubbish idea. My voice is going and my throat hurts,' Moin croaked crossly. He was really fed up. 'When *I* needed to sing, the

monster sang and everyone got angry. When the *monster* was supposed to sing, I had to sing, and now again everyone will be angry. It's not fair!'

The monster jumped on to the bed, stood on a pile of pillows and sang:

Life is not fair
Who said it was?
When you want to fast-forward
Life wants to pause.
When you want it sunny
Life wants to rain.
Oh life is not fair
It's often a pain.

'With you around, it's *always* a pain,' said Moin.

Magic Potion

If Mr and Mrs Kaif had been at home when the car came to drop off Loopy's magic potion, it would not have happened.

If Moin had listened to Tony and drunk the magic potion himself, it would not have happened.

If he had listened to Parvati and thrown it away, it would not have happened.

But Mr and Mrs Kaif were out, and Tony was with Moin, when a car came and dropped off the medicine. The label said: Magic Potion. The driver said, 'Loopy-saab has sent this for the singer boy. Three teaspoons a day, for three days.'

'What's it for?' Tony asked the driver.

'For khich-khich in the throat,' said the driver and laughed maniacally.

That should have warned them. It didn't.

'That's pretty nice of Loopy,' Tony remarked. 'He must have realised you'd strained your voice.'

Moin nodded. His voice had gone completely.

'So drink it,' said Tony.

Moin shook his head. He wasn't going to drink anything that Loopy had sent. Not without being sure what was in it.

Tony Skyped Parvati to help him convince Moin to drink the medicine.

'Moin!' said Parvati, wagging her finger

warningly, '*do not drink it*. Throw it away at once.'

Moin nodded and signed off Skype.

'Why did you put her off?' asked the monster. 'I was going to sing my new song. I wanted her to hear.'

Moin signed that no one wanted to hear the new song.

'You're going to strangle yourself?' asked the monster. He clearly didn't understand Moin's sign language.

Moin growled. It was the only noise he could manage—a low, wordless growl, deep in his throat.

'Is that your new voice? Nah. I don't like it. Okay, let me sing you this song I've composed.'

Moin shook his head vigorously. But the monster struck a pose and was about to begin. Moin quickly gave it Loopy's magic potion.

'What's this?' asked the monster.

'Hey! That's not for you,' Tony cried. 'That's the magic potion sent by Loopy Bagiri to help Moin get his voice back.'

'I want to drink magic potion,' said the monster.

'It'll make my voice even better. What flavour is it?'

'Doesn't say,' said Tony. 'But you'd better not drink it. Remember what happened when you drank Moin's deworming medicine? If you've forgotten, I can read it out for you— it's in my book. And remember rule 321? You don't know—'

MONSTER RULE 321

Human products can have unpredictable side effects on monsters.

But the monster had emptied the bottle in one gulp.

If Mrs Kooki had not convinced Kooki that the thing he saw at Moin's house was just a piece of paper, it would not have happened.

If Kooki and Mrs Kooki had not come to Moin's house to confirm this, it would not have happened.

But Mr and Mrs Kaif were not at home, Moin had got the magic potion, he had not listened to Tony or to Parvati, Mrs Kooki had convinced Kooki that the pink thing was a piece of paper, and at the very moment that the monster swallowed a bottleful of Loopy Bagiri's magic potion, the doorbell in Moin's house rang.

Tony and Moin didn't know what to do. They needed to keep an eye on the monster, and they needed to answer the doorbell. They would have to split up. Moin, being voiceless, would have to watch the monster, while Tony dealt with the door.

Tony ran to the door and opened it.

'Anh, Tony, you are here!' said Kooki.

'Hello!' beamed Mrs Kooki.

The next moment, both Kooki and his wife had been knocked flat by something that zipped over Tony's head and out the door.

'Catch it!' Moin tried to yell, running after the thing, but all that came from is throat was a strangled sound. Tony hopped over his prone principal and ran after the pinkish blur, with Moin in hot pursuit.

The monster whizzed up to the main road,

then turned around and whizzed past Tony and Moin in the opposite direction. Tony and Moin screeched to a halt, turned around and began to run after it again.

'Do you think it's going back home?' Tony panted.

'Grrrrrr?' Moin croaked back.

Turned out it wasn't. For the next few minutes, the monster zipped from one end of the street to the other, buzzing like a hive of bees. A crowd began to gather. Someone called the police control room.

'There is a thing flying in our street!' he said.

'So?' asked the bored operator, chewing on her fifth chocolate bar of the day. She had had three useless calls already. One about a cat stuck in a garbage bin, one about a UFO, which on close questioning turned out to be a crow, and one about a girl screaming in a neighbouring house, which she could clearly recognise, even through the phone, as Loopy Bagiri's latest hit song.

A random 'thing' flying through someone's street was, as far as she was concerned, the last straw.

'Ahanh? What kind of *thing*?' she asked in her most sarcastic voice.

'It's a sort of ... er ... pink ... er ... thing,' stuttered the man.

'Could it be a bird, do you think?' asked the operator. 'You know that birds fly, right? That's what they do. It's not against the law.'

'It's not a bird!' the man yelled.

'Right. What *is* it then?'

'I don't know.'

'Describe it?'

'It's pink.'

'And?'

'It's … a … sort of …a … shapeless blur.'

'So you want me to ask the nearest police station to come and arrest a shapeless blur? On what grounds? Because shapelessness is now a criminal offence?' She chomped viciously on the last of her chocolate bar.

'I'm sick and tired of people calling for useless, pointless things!' she shouted. 'Has there been a robbery? Call us! Has there been a murder? Call us, and we'll come running! But don't call to tell us about birds and butterflies and pink, shapeless things flying through the air, understand? It's alright to be shapeless. Everyone can't be Kapeera Kanoor!!'

The man stared at his phone in shock.

The crowd, meanwhile, had grown and was buzzing louder than the monster was. The monster showed no signs of slowing down, which, as far as Tony and Moin were concerned, was a good thing. Because once it did, and people saw it, they had no idea what would happen.

But as the crowd got bigger, they realised that something would have to be done. Any moment now, one or more of several things would happen: the monster would stop whizzing and buzzing; the police would come and catch them for disturbing the peace; Moin's parents would come back.

But what happened was the one possibility they'd forgotten about.

Kooki and his wife got up, dazed, and looked around. They saw Moin and Tony running up and down behind a buzzing thing and before their eyes, the crowd grew and grew.

At first, they felt like leaving it all and going home. As they turned to go, Kooki looked back and saw Moin and Tony at the edge of the crowd, looking very small and scared. Kooki and Mrs Kooki had been teachers for many years. They had a strong sense of responsibility towards children, even children who unleashed strange things on them and jumped over them as they lay winded.

'Teacher, we cannot leave them,' Kooki told his wife.

'You're right, Sir. Whatever is going on, we have to help them.'

Hawaldar Jeevan Kumar had joined the police force for several reasons. First of all, he thought he would look good in uniform. Secondly, he liked the idea of being a hero, catching thieves, and getting medals. Thirdly, when he imagined helping old people and children and animals, it gave him a nice, warm feeling.

The only trouble was, he hated loud, angry voices. When people shouted, he began to tremble, and tears came to his eyes. This was proving to be a big problem in his job.

People who came into the police station were always shouting. People who were robbed came and shouted that no one was protecting their homes, people whose children had run away shouted that the police were not trying to find them, gangsters came and yelled threats, and the senior policemen were always screaming at the junior policemen. As a result, Jeevan Kumar, or JK, as he was known to his colleagues and friends, was permanently trembling and teary-eyed.

Finally, JK had opted for traffic duty. It was hot, tiring work, but people didn't yell abuses and threats at him. At least, not all the time. There was the odd drunken driver, and once a little lady on a scooter, who had cut the traffic light, had screamed at him for stopping her. He had let her go quickly, because she had told him that she had a bad case of the runs and needed to get home at once. (He did wish she had not called him a langur, though. He was sensitive about his looks.)

But those were exceptions. Usually the only noise he had to deal with was the honking of horns, the screeching of brakes and the occasional blaring of music in cars that sped by carrying nasty young people who thought they owned the roads because they were rich.

Today, however, he noticed that there was a new kind of noise in the air. It started with a strange buzz, like a hundred bees gone mad. Then gradually, it was mixed with a more familiar buzz, the buzz of many human voices.

Across the road, at the entrance to one of the quiet residential streets, he saw that a crowd was gathering. Soon it would spill on to the main road and block traffic.

Hawaldar Jeevan Kumar was a young man with a strong sense of duty. He called the nearby police station for someone to take his place at the traffic signal, and set off to find out what was causing the commotion in the street.

As he neared the thickest part of the crowd, there was a sudden heaving, as if someone had lit a firecracker in the middle of it. He couldn't see what had caused it, but the crowd started rushing away.

When the crowd thinned, he saw a small woman waving a black umbrella around. He recognised the woman on the scooter who had called him a langur and his throat went dry.

But he plodded on, remembering that it was his duty to help the public.

'Go! Go! All you stupid, staring people! Go!' she was shouting.

On the other side of the street, there was a man who seemed to be giving some sort of speech to the crowd.

'It is very bad manners, enh,' Kooki was telling a bunch of very confused people. 'These two children are just playing with some toy, and you are all standing and staring and scaring them. This is very reprehensible, very bad. I request you, therefore, to kindly go home and stare at something in your house. You have television, stare at that. Otherwise, stare at your husband or wife or even mother or father. Or, if you don't want to do that, stare out of the window. You can stare at passing cars and scooters, you can stare at the trees or electric poles. No need to stand here and frighten small children. Please go home.'

Mrs Kooki's method was clearly more effective. Her side of the street cleared up miraculously. She went over to Kooki's side and within seconds, the street was clear. That was when Mrs Kooki saw Hawaldar Jeevan Kumar trotting up.

'Ah, now you come!' she said. 'So the Hindi movies are very correct, huh? The police always come after everything is over! What is the use? Where were you when the crowd was here? Go home now! Go!' she shouted at JK.

JK stood still. His ears went red and began to tremble—the trembling always started with his ears. His eyes filled up.

'I … I …' he said, but Mrs Kooki had suddenly recognised him.

'Oh, you are that traffic policeman!' she said, calming down at once. 'Sir, this is the kind policeman who let me go that time when my stomach was upset.'

Kooki came over and pumped JK's limp hand up and down.

'Thank you very much, sir!' he said to JK. 'It was very good of you to let my wife go. She was in very great discomfort, you know.'

JK sniffed and wiped his eyes.

'It is our duty to help the public, sir,' he said, with a watery smile. 'Wh-what was going on here?' he asked, a little afraid that the little lady would start shouting again.

'There was a big crowd terrorising these two—' began Kooki, but when he turned around, he realised that Tony and Moin were missing, and so was the buzzing thing.

As they wondered where the children had disappeared, they heard a voice from inside the house:

A spoonful of medicine
Like sugar going down
Sugar going down
Sugar going down

A spoonful of medicine
Like sugar going down
Makes me want to fade away.

Kooki stood rooted to the spot. It was the sweetest voice he had ever heard.

'We have done our duty, Sir,' said Mrs Kooki with quiet pride. 'The children are safely home. We can go now.'

As Hawaldar Jeevan Kumar made his way back to his post at the traffic signal, he wished he had joined the postal service, like his father before him. They got bitten by excited dogs sometimes, but nobody shouted at postmen.

Back in the house, a strange thing was happening. With every line the monster sang in its newly sweet voice, it was getting lighter and lighter. Soon it had turned a pale pink and was floating up in the air.

'What's going on?' cried Tony. 'I told you not to drink the magic potion. I told you anything could happen!'

The monster sang, its voice growing fainter and fainter:

Like sugar in a cup of tea
I'm no longer me.
I'm dissolving and fading
Floating free,
And soon I might no longer be
I won't see you and you won't see—

And the monster disappeared.
    'Oh no!' said Tony.
    'It'll be back,' croaked Moin, refusing to
believe his luck.

Anushka Ravishankar is a children's writer based in Delhi. She has written over twenty books for children, many of which have received international awards. Her books include the *Zain and Ana* series, *Elephants Never Forget, Song of the Bookworm* and *To Market! To Market!* Several of her books have been translated into Dutch, German, Italian, Spanish and other languages.

Anitha Balachandran makes a precarious living as a award-winning animation film-maker and illustrator. Her work has been exhibited and published internationally. Her present preoccupations include stories about animals, stories for and about children and of old people. You might pass her in the street if you happen to be in Delhi.